# Doctor

Lucy M. George          Ando Twin

527 804 47 6

Doctor Miranda works in a GP practice.

She helps make people better
when they feel ill or have been hurt.

"Good morning, Doctor!"
says the receptionist.

"You have lots of people to see.
It's going to be a busy day!"

Doctor Miranda's first patient has a swollen ankle.

"Oh dear, Olivia. Can I have a look?"
asks Doctor Miranda gently.

She feels Olivia's leg and ankle,
asking her where it hurts the most.

Doctor Miranda thinks Olivia needs an X-ray.
She tells Olivia's mummy to take her to the hospital.

"Just to make sure nothing's broken!"
says Doctor Miranda.

Next, Doctor Miranda gives twin babies their injections...

...sees a boy with a bad case of chickenpox...

...checks a pregnant woman's blood pressure...

...and listens to a man's chest with her stethoscope.

Now Doctor Miranda has to call patients
who are too poorly to leave home.

She asks them questions and
then decides how to help them.

Doctor Miranda is about to go and have lunch when the receptionist rushes in.

"Can you see one more patient this morning, Doctor?" she asks.

Jimmy has just arrived at the surgery for an emergency appointment.

His daddy explains that he has a cough and a high temperature.

Doctor Miranda asks whether Jimmy has a rash or any other symptoms.

"No, he's just been sleeping lots today, haven't you, Jimmy?" his daddy says.

Doctor Miranda takes
Jimmy's temperature
with a thermometer.

Then she looks
in his ears with
an otoscope.

"Say ahh!"
she tells Jimmy.

"Ahhhhh!" Jimmy
says, opening
his mouth wide.

Then she looks
at the back of
his throat using
a special stick.

Next, Doctor Miranda
asks Jimmy to sit
on the bed
and take off
his jumper.

Doctor Miranda listens carefully to Jimmy's chest using a stethoscope.

It feels cold and it tickles!

Doctor Miranda thinks Jimmy
has a chest infection.

She writes him a prescription for some
medicine and asks him to come back
in a couple of days if he's not better.

"You should feel well again very soon," she tells him, waving goodbye.

"Thank you, Doctor," says Jimmy.

Doctor Miranda
checks her
afternoon schedule
with the receptionist.

What a busy day it's been already!

Doctor Miranda just has to make one more call...

...before she can go out for lunch!

# What else does Doctor Miranda do?

Visits patients at home.

Sends people to hospital.

Gives injections to stop people getting ill.

Gives people their test results.

# What does Doctor Miranda need?

Stethoscope

Computer

Prescription pad

Telephone

Tongue depressors

Otoscope

Thermometer

# Other busy people

Here are some of the other busy people doctors work with.

**Receptionists** book appointments for patients, get test results from the hospital and look after patient records.

**Pharmacists** are highly trained and know all about medicines. They make up prescriptions and also give health advice.

**Nurses** care for wounds, give health advice, take blood for tests and treat other non-serious ailments.

**Ambulance drivers** take people who are very ill or injured to the hospital so they can see a doctor quickly.

# Next steps

- In the story, Doctor Miranda sees lots of patients with different problems. Ask the children what they thought of Doctor Miranda's day.

- Doctor Miranda was very caring throughout the day. Ask the children what other qualities a doctor should have. Would any of them like to be a doctor?

- Doctor Miranda has lots of special equipment. Ask the children if they remember what any of it was called or what it was used for. Discuss any equipment the children might have come across themselves.

- Ask the children if they remember being ill or visiting the doctor. How did they feel? What helped them to feel better?

- Talk to the children about the other busy people in the book and whether they have met any of them. What else do they know about these jobs? What would the children like to be when they grow up?

Quarto is the authority on a wide range of topics.
Quarto educates, entertains and enriches the lives of our readers—enthusiasts and lovers of hands-on living.
www.quartoknows.com

Publisher: Zeta Jones
Associate Publisher: Maxime Boucknooghe
Editorial Director: Victoria Garrard
Art Director: Laura Roberts-Jensen
Editor: Sophie Hallam
Designer: Anna Lubecka

Copyright © QED Publishing 2015

First published in the UK in 2015 by
QED Publishing
Part of The Quarto Group,
The Old Brewery, 6 Blundell Street, London, N7 9BH

A catalogue record for this book is available from the British Library.

ISBN 978 1 78493 152 0

Printed in the UK

MIX
Paper from responsible sources
FSC® C013604

For Granny Wilson
- AndoTwin

For Islay & Donald
- Lucy M. George